Hush, Hush!

Margaret Wild & Bridget Strevens-Marzo

LITTLE HARE

www.littleharebooks.com

For Quinn – MW

For my parents, John and Julia Strevens, in loving memory – BS-M

Little Hare Books
8/21 Mary Street, Surry Hills NSW 2010
AUSTRALIA www.littleharebooks.com
Copyright © text Margaret Wild 2009
Copyright © illustrations Bridget Strevens-Marzo 2009
First published 2009 All rights reserved. No part of this
publication may be reproduced, stored in a retrieval
system or transmitted in any form or by any means, electronic,
mechanical, photocopying, recording or otherwise,
without the prior written permission of the publisher.
National Library of Australia Cataloguing-in-Publication
entry Wild, Margaret, 1948- Hush, hush! / Margaret Wild ;
illustrator, Bridget Strevens-Marzo. 9781921272868 (hbk.)
For pre-school age. Strevens-Marzo, Bridget.
A823.3 Designed by Bernadette Gethings
Produced by Pica Digital, Singapore
Printed in China through Phoenix
Offset 54321

Baby Hippo couldn't fall asleep.

He rolled and wriggled.

He stood on his head. He waggled his legs.

He grunted and groaned. "Oh, ah, oh!"

"Hush, hush!" said his *mum* softly and sleepily.
But Baby Hippo couldn't hush.

So he got up and went for a walk.
Through the rippling, rustling reeds trotted Baby Hippo.
And this is what he heard...

"Hush, hush!"

Along the soggy, boggy mud trotted Baby Hippo.
And this is what he heard...

"Hush, hush!"

Over the lumpy, humpy rocks trotted Baby Hippo.
And this is what he heard...

"Hush, hush!"

Through the willowy, wavy grass trotted Baby Hippo.
And this is what he heard...

"Hush, hush!"

Under the shady, shadowy trees trotted Baby Hippo.
And this is what he heard...

"Hush, hush!"

Baby Hippo yawned. He could hardly keep his eyes open.

Baby Hippo trudged back under the shady, shadowy trees,

through the willowy, wavy grass,

over the lumpy, humpy rocks,

along the soggy, boggy mud,

through the rippling, rustling reeds, back to his *mum.*

Baby Hippo snuggled up to her and closed his eyes.
He was just about to fall asleep when this is what he heard...

"Snort, snore! Snort, snore!"
"Hush, hush!" said Baby Hippo softly and sleepily.

But Mum couldn't hush.

"Grunt, groan, gruffle!" she said in her sleep. "Snort, snore, snuffle!"

"Snort, snuffle, snore!" said Baby Hippo.